WOULD YOU MAIL A HIPPO?

Library of Congress Cataloging-in-Publication Data

Woodworth, Viki.
Would you mail a hippo? / Viki Woodworth.
p. cm
Summary: Silly rhymes introduce what goes on at such places
in a community as the library, post office, grocery store and school.
ISBN 1-56766-179-3
[1. City and town life—Fiction. 2. Stories in rhyme.]
1. Title.
PZ8.3.W893W1 1995   94-45828
[E]—dc20   CIP / AC

WOULD YOU MAIL A HIPPO?

Written and Illustrated by
Viki Woodworth

Viki Woodworth and family.

What do you borrow from the library?

A boat?
A book?

A skunk
or canary?

A Book

Which would you buy at a grocery store?

**Bread or
a door?**

Bread

At a post office, what would you see?

A clown?
A letter?

A hippo
or tree?

A Letter

What do you see
in every
school?

A lion?
A car?

A teacher
or a mule?

A Teacher

We have these places
in our community

to make
things easier

for you
and for me.